ME ENCANTA EL BÉISBOL/
I LOVE BASEBALL

By Ryan Nagelhout   Traducido por Eida de la Vega

Gareth Stevens
PUBLISHING

Please visit our website, www.garethstevens.com. For a free color catalog of all our high-quality books, call toll free 1-800-542-2595 or fax 1-877-542-2596.

Library of Congress Cataloging-in-Publication Data

Nagelhout, Ryan.
I love baseball = Me encanta el béisbol / by Ryan Nagelhout.
 p. cm. — (My favorite sports = Mis deportes favoritos)
Parallel title: Mis deportes favoritos
In English and Spanish.
Includes index.
ISBN 978-1-4824-0846-1 (library binding)
1. Baseball — Juvenile literature. I. Nagelhout, Ryan. II. Title.
GV867.5 N34 2015
796.357—d23

First Edition

Published in 2015 by
Gareth Stevens Publishing
111 East 14th Street, Suite 349
New York, NY 10003

Editor: Ryan Nagelhout
Designer: Nick Domiano
Spanish Translation: Eida de la Vega

Photo credits: Cover, p. 1 Zoran Milich/Allsport Concepts/Getty Images; pp. 5, 19, 24 (base, bat) Stockbyte/Thinkstock.com; p. 7 MikeC123/Shutterstock.com; p. 9, 24 (glove) sonya etchison/Shutterstock.com; p. 11 Pete Pahham/Shutterstock.com; p. 13 Comstock Images/Thinkstock.com; pp. 15, 24 (bat) Cheryl Ann Quigley/Shutterstock.com; p. 17 Monkey Business Images/Shutterstock.com; p. 21 tammykayphoto/Shutterstock.com; p. 23 Creatas Images/Thinkstock.com.

Printed in the United States of America

CPSIA compliance information: Batch #CS15GS: For further information contact Gareth Stevens, New York, New York at 1-800-542-2595S

Contenido

- -

Contents

¡Me encanta el béisbol!

I love baseball!

Es muy divertido.

It is fun to play.

El guante que uso es
de cuero. Es un guante
de béisbol.

I wear a leather mitt
on my hand.
This is called a glove.

Me ayuda a atrapar
la pelota.

It helps me catch
the ball.

Me encanta lanzar
la pelota.

I love throwing
a baseball.

Me gusta batear
la pelota.

I like to hit the ball.

Uso un bate
de madera.

I use a wooden bat.

Trato de batear
un jonrón.

I try to hit a home run.

Me gusta recorrer
las bases.

I like to run the bases.

21

¿Te gusta el béisbol?

Do you like baseball?

23

Palabras que debes saber/ Words to Know

la base/
base

el bate/
bat

el guante/
glove

Índice / Index